Giddy-up, uh-oh! Wheels are draggin'.

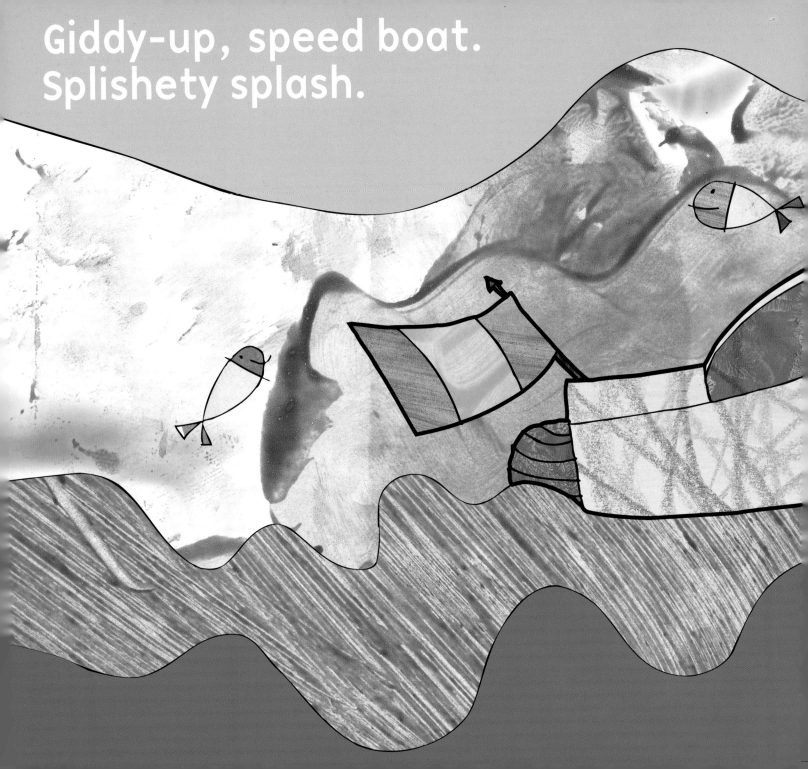

Giddy-up, speed boat.
Splishety splash.

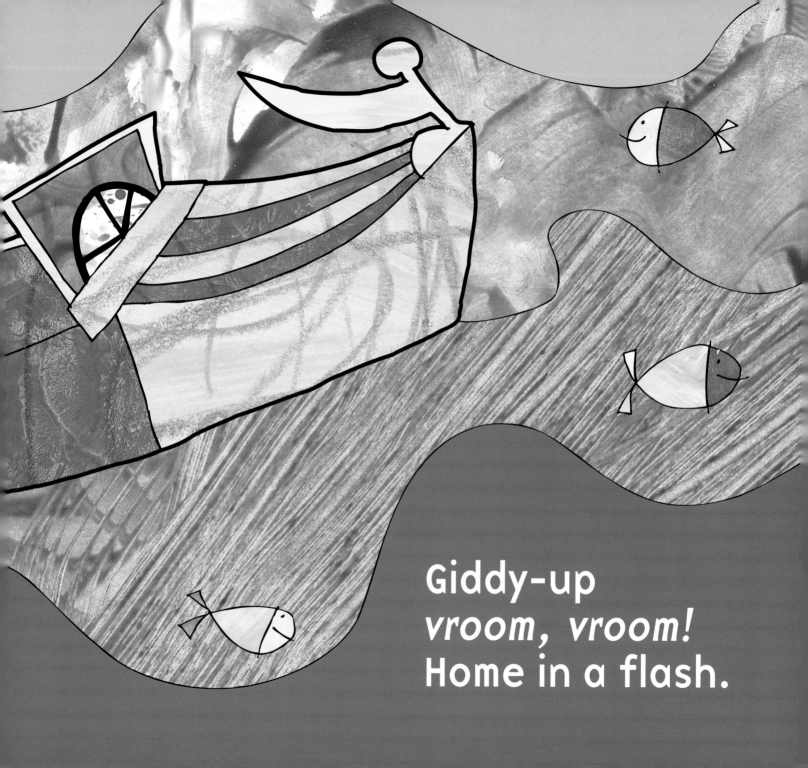

Giddy-up
vroom, vroom!
Home in a flash.

Giddy-up, race car,
on a racetrack.

Giddy-up around,
and giddy on back.

Giddy-up, airplane,
into the sky.

Giddy-up higher.
My, oh my!

Giddy-up, bus,
in the big, big city.

Stop, bus! Go, bus!
Giddy, giddy, giddy!

Giddy-up FAST, and blow your horn!

Giddy-up, Sammy,
Nana and Pop.

Kindermusik
Our time

away we Go!

Special thanks to the Kindermusik International employees and families who had so much fun painting the paper for *Giddy-Up!*

Manufactured by MidAtlantic Printers
Altavista, VA USA
October 31, 2017
21127/96882

Dena C. Adams
Marlin Adams
Micah Adams
Heather Balent
Sabrina Balent
Jon Balent
Vanessa Balent
Michael Blackburn
Christie Bo
Devan Bolder

Augusta Bedwell
Robert Bedwell
Casean Clay
Helen Brauner
Amy Brown
Cindy Bousm

Cynthia Dougherty
Ellie Dougherty
Frances Dougherty
Michael Dougherty
Sarah Dougherty
Danielle Davis
Christie Bolden
Devan Bolden
Susan Hanford
Robert Docke
Christy Docker
Morgan Eastlac

Angie Gates
Shelley Fincher
Terry Fincher
Susan James

Shawn Hyatt
Jesse Hoggard
Josie Hoggard
J.P. Hauman
Kurtys Haumann

Carmi Medoff
Kristen Kinsey
Luke Kinsey
Michelle Kinsey
Scott Kinsey
Cristi Phillips
David McMillin
Vickie McM
Heather May

David Williams
Martha Williams
Noah Williams
Rheva Williams
Kim Shue
Nichole Smith
Wendy Smith
Andy Smith
Sandra St

From the **Kindermusik** Library

w w w . k i n d e r m u s i k . c o m
©1999 Kindermusik® International, Inc.
2606 Phoenix Drive Suite 810, Greensboro, N.C. 27406, U.S.A.
1-02-02010 ISBN:0-945613-77-6